THIS IS SOCCER

For Pati Netto in Rio, for Fred Milgram on Nantucket, and always, for Dash Lunde in New York City   — M.B.

For Tess   — J.O'B.

Henry Holt and Company, Inc., *Publishers since 1866*, 115 West 18th Street, New York, New York 10011

Henry Holt is a registered trademark of Henry Holt and Company, Inc.

Library of Congress Cataloging-in-Publication Data
Blackstone, Margaret. This is soccer / by Margaret Blackstone; illustrated by John O'Brien.
Summary: A simple introduction to the game of soccer, covering its equipment, players, and basic plays
and depicting a game in progress.
1. Soccer—Juvenile literature. [1. Soccer.] I. O'Brien, John, ill. II. Title. GV943.25.B52 1999 796.334—dc21 98-23474

ISBN 0-8050-2801-3 / First Edition—1999 / Printed in the United States of America on acid-free paper. ∞
The illustrator used watercolor on bristol paper to create the illustrations for this book.
10 9 8 7 6 5 4 3 2 1

THIS IS SOCCER

Margaret Blackstone   illustrated by **John O'Brien**

Henry Holt and Company • New York

This is a soccer ball.

This is a cleat.

And this is a soccer player.

In soccer you lead with your feet,
think on your feet,
wobble, topple,
and dance with your feet.

This footwork is
called dribbling.

This footwork is
called juggling.

This player doesn't know which foot is which.

This is one soccer team,

and this is another.

This is a kickoff.

And this is a pass.

Heads turn this way and that,
upfield, downfield,
    eyes left, eyes right.

This player plays offense.

This is a long shot.

This player plays defense.

This is a save.

And this is the crowd shouting,

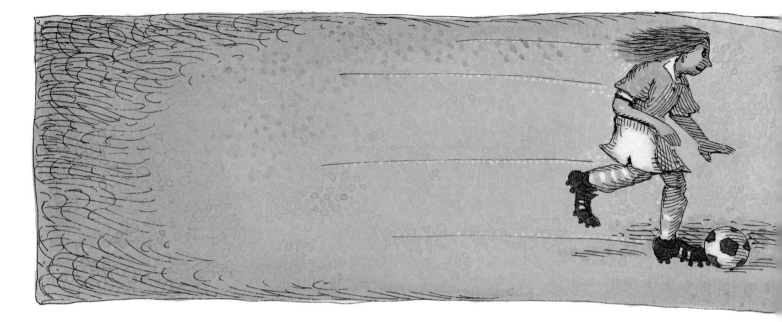

Soccer is a game of long runs and short stops,

quick turns, even grass burns.

When the ball's too high
for the fleetest of feet,
heads join the dance,
butting the ball
with a leap
and a soar.

Only the goalie can use his hands, as he
keeps the ball as far from his goal as he can.

A soccer player is always in motion,
running and jumping,
bumping and sliding,

falling low, flying high,
  not stopping, just going.

Dribble, pass, pass, dribble,

faster, faster, dribble, pass—

KICK!

This is an overhead shot.

And this

is a goal!

In soccer there's always more shooting than scoring.
At the end of the game the score may be so low
that it's still zero to zero.

Some people find this boring.
Those are the ones you'll usually see snoring,
when everyone else is roaring.

Soccer is played around the world,
from New York City to Katmandu.

Soccer is always fun,
but soccer is *most* fun
when it's played by me and you.

Bag Book